ISBN 0 86163 101 3

First published in 1952 by Brockhampton Press Limited in
Lucky Story Book

This edition first published in 1984 by
AWARD PUBLICATIONS LIMITED
SPRING HOUSE, SPRING PLACE
LONDON NW5

Reprinted 1985

Printed in Belgium

Enid Blyton

THE BONFIRE FOLK

Illustrated by Suzy-Jane Tanner

AWARD PUBLICATIONS

THE BONFIRE FOLK

PETER and Jean were running home from school one day when they passed the cobbler's shop. Mr Knock the cobbler was sitting cross-legged in his window, mending somebody's shoes.

His glass window was closed, for it was a cold day. Peter knocked on it, for he and Jean always liked to have a smile from the old cobbler. He had eyes as blue as forget-me-nots, and whiskers as white as snow.

Mr Knock looked up and smiled. Then he beckoned the children inside. They opened the door and walked in, sniffing the good smell of leather.

'Did you want us, Mr Knock?' asked Peter.

'Yes,' said Mr Knock. 'I want to know if you'll do an old man a good turn. My boy's ill and there are three pairs of shoes to be sent out. Do you think you and Jean could leave them for me on your way home?'

'Of course, Mr Knock,' said Peter. 'We'd love to. Where are they?'

The old cobbler gave three parcels to them. 'That's for Captain Brown,' he said. 'That's for Mrs Lee — and that little one is for Mrs George's baby. You know where they all live, don't you?'

'Yes, Mr Knock!' said the children, pleased. It was fun to play at being errand-boys! They rushed off with the parcels and left them at the right houses. Then they went home to lunch. On their way to afternoon school, they went to see Mr Knock again.

'We left all your parcels safely for you,' said Peter.

'Thank you kindly,' said Mr Knock. 'Now what would you like for a reward?'

'Nothing!' said Jean at once. 'We did it for you because we like you. We don't want to be paid.'

'Well, I won't pay you,' said Mr Knock, his blue eyes shining. 'But I happen to know something you badly want and maybe I'll be able to help you to get it. I know that you want to see the fairy folk, don't you?'

'Oooh, yes,' said both children at once. 'But we never have.'

'Well, I'll tell you a time *I* saw them,' said Mr Knock, almost in a whisper. 'I saw them one cold December night, my dears — all toasting themselves beside my father's bonfire at the bottom of the garden. I've never told anyone till today — but now I'm telling you, for maybe you'll see them there too!'

Well! The children were so surprised that they could hardly say a word. They went off to school full of excitement. Daddy was at home that day and meant to make a bonfire. Suppose, just suppose, they saw the little folk round the flames?

They went down to look at the bonfire after school. Daddy said he was going to let it out soon and the children were disappointed. They ran off to some woods nearby and, in the half-dark, managed to find some dry fir-cones. 'We'll use these to keep the fire in after tea,' said Jean. 'They burn beautifully.'

They placed a little pile of them beside the still-burning fire and ran in to tea — but afterwards, Auntie Mollie came and the two children had to stay and talk to her. It was their bedtime, before they could think of going down to the bonfire again.

'Let's creep down now and see if anyone is there,' said Jean. 'I *would* so like to see. It's very cold and frosty tonight — maybe there will be one or two of the little folk there already.'

Jean and Peter put on their coats, their hats and their scarves. They opened the garden door softly, and crept down the garden, walking on the grass so that their feet should make no noise.

'The bonfire is still burning,' whispered Jean. 'It didn't go out after all. Can you see anyone there?'

The children went round a hedge and came in sight of the fire. It was burning brightly and the smoke swirled away from it, smelling delicious. Jean and Peter stopped and looked.

'There's Whiskers, our cat, sitting by it!' said Jean in a delighted whisper. 'And look — there's the cat next door too! Both warming their toes!'

'What's that the other side?' whispered back Peter. 'I think — I really do think it's a brownie!'

It was! He was a tiny little man with a long beard and twinkling eyes. He was throwing fir-cones on the fire. No wonder it was burning brightly!

'It's the fir-cones we collected!' said Jean. 'How lovely! Oh, look — here's someone coming!

Somebody came out of the shadowy bushes and sat down by the fire. It was an elf with long shining wings. She spoke to the cats and the brownie and they all nodded to her. They knew one another, it was quite certain. The fairy had brought some bundles of small twigs with her and these she threw on the fire every now and again, making it burn even more brightly.

Then a hedgehog came and a rabbit. They sat down by the bonfire and the rabbit held out both his paws to the flames. Jean and Peter thought he looked lovely.

'Isn't this exciting?' whispered Jean. 'I never thought we'd see all this! Do you suppose everybody's bonfires have bonfire folk around them at night?'

'I expect so,' said Peter. 'Oh, Jean — do let's go and speak to them all! I'm sure they won't be frightened.'

The two children left the hedge they were standing by and walked softly to the bonfire. Nobody saw them at first — and then the two cats pricked up their ears, spied them both and shot away like shadows.

Peter caught hold of the brownie and held him tightly. 'Don't be afraid,' he said. 'I just want to speak to you. This is our bonfire and we are so pleased to see you. Come and warm yourselves by it. I am glad you used the fir-cones to make it burn brightly.'

'Oh, did *you* leave the fir-cones?' said the brownie. 'How kind of you! The fire was nearly out but the dry cones just got it going again nicely. You're sure you don't mind us warming ourselves here? It's so very cold tonight — and these garden bonfires are so useful to us little folk.'

'You come whenever you like,' said Peter, letting go the brownie, now that the little man knew the children were friends. For a few minutes they all sat there together and the rabbit was just about to jump on to Jean's knee, when the children heard their mother calling.

'Peter! Jean! You naughty children! Surely you haven't gone out into the cold garden! Come to bed at once.'

'Goodbye!' said the children to the bonfire folk. 'Tell everybody to use our fire each night. We like to know you are there.' And off they ran to bed.

They love to think of all the little bonfire-folk sitting round the smoky fire in the garden. Do *you* ever have a bonfire? Well, maybe the little folk are round yours, too, warming their toes on a winter's evening! Wouldn't I love to see them!